OEDIPUS IN JERUSALEM

OEDIPUS IN JERUSALEM

A Play in Two Acts

Kalman J. Kaplan

Foreword by
J. Harold Ellens

RESOURCE *Publications* • Eugene, Oregon

OEDIPUS IN JERUSALEM
A Play in Two Acts

Resource Publications
An Imprint of Wipf and Stock Publishers
199 W. 8th Ave., Suite 3
Eugene, OR 97401

www.wipfandstock.com

ISBN 13: 978-1-4982-2915-9

Manufactured in the U.S.A.   08/11/2015

To my parents, Lewis C. Kaplan and Edith Saposnik Kaplan, who raised me with love and enabled me to understand that I can overcome life's obstacles, to my son Daniel Lewis Kaplan, whom I hope I have raised the same way, and finally, to Moriah Markus-Kaplan who has deepened my understanding of life immeasurably and provided her home in Tel Aviv for the beginning of the composition of the this play.

Acknowledgments

The author would like to acknowledge the comments and insights provided by Professor Michael Shapiro, Dr. Matthew Schwartz, Dr. Daniel Silverfarb, Isabelle Proton, Esq., Mr. Yaron Iram and Ms. Lisa Collins with regard to various drafts of this play. Michael read an early draft and supplied very useful comments on the structure of the play. Matthew provided a great deal of information regarding the actual workings of the Sanhedrin. Daniel brought the perspective of a trial attorney to the courtroom scenes. Isabelle immediately grasped the sense of Oedipus being an "unwanted child."

The yeoman work of Lori Thompson and Israel "Izzy" Cohen must also be acknowledged. Lori was always alert to subtle nuances in the dialogue which made this play much stronger. Izzy provided invaluable assistance with proofreading and formatting. This work benefited very much from their efforts.

The author must also acknowledge Sophocles' great play, *Oedipus Rex*. We have abridged small passages of dialogue from the translation by R. C. Jebb in W. S. Oates and E. O'Neill, Jr. (Eds.), 1938, The Complete Greek Tragedy, Volume 1, pp. 369–422. New York: Random House.

Foreword

Dr. Kalman Kaplan, a Professor of Clinical Psychology, presents us with a two act play built upon the frame of a work by Sophocles. The latter was a famed Greek playwright of the fifth century BCE. In fact, he lived for almost that entire century. His fame lay both in his remarkably positive civic service and accomplishments, and also in the fact that he won more prizes than the other dramatists of his time, including Aeschylus and Euripides. These three frequently competed for the prize at the annual Athenian festivals. Sophocles wrote 123 plays for the competition. The first time Sophocles won was in 468, when he defeated Aeschylus for the prize.

The most famous of Sophocles' works is *Oedipus the King*. In his play, Oedipus is caught in the trap set by the fateful gods, unwittingly killing his father and committing incest with his mother. Upon discovering the truth, he blinds himself out of shame and to avoid seeing his parents in the afterworld. He is confined to the Palace until the oracles can be consulted, though they have driven him to this tragic destiny by their messages of blind fate.

Kaplan redesigns the structure of Sophocles' tragedy, presenting the play with a new story line, plot, thrust and denouement. The characters essentially remain the same, but for the addition of the Hebrew prophet, Nathan, of biblical note, who brings Oedipus, the fated king, to Jerusalem for a trial by the Sanhedrin. Here the intrigue and tension of the play elevates and accelerates. As the courtroom drama adds new dimensions to the original play, *Oedipus in Jerusalem*, takes on a stirring twist. Kaplan's whole intent is to set in tension and contrast not only two perspectives on Oedipus' destiny, but the dramatic difference between two world-views,

Greek and Hebrew, in ancient times and ours today. This involves comparing the theologies about the nature of God, codes of justice, methods of juridical procedure and, especially, comprehensive world-views both in the ancient world and the world today.

The play is set against the backdrop of a long cultural history. The historic Greek philosophical world-view is famous for such figures as Pythagoras, Plato, Aristotle, the Sophists, the Epicureans, and even Philo Judaeus, Plotinus, and Porphyry. Historically, that cultural history boiled down to the idealism of Platonism and the practical empiricism of Aristotelianism. These world views largely shaped the world from the fifth century B.C.E. to our own time. Kaplan sets this world-view over against the trial of Oedipus in Jerusalem. The outcome is a twist, a surprise, a definitive destiny that the entire chaotic world must take account of in our day. Kaplan brings a piece of history to the table that we must pay attention to, in order to overcome our entrapment by fate and the disaster of a self-fulfilling prophecy, facing us this very minute.

The Rev. Dr. J. Harold Ellens

Preface

Our contemporary understanding of Oedipus has been so shaped, indeed somewhat misshaped, by Freud's postulation of the *oedipus complex*, that we reflexively think of Oedipus as a man who knowingly killed his father to possess his mother. Indeed, that he was motivated to do so.

There are certainly other characters in Greek mythology that display this pattern. For example, Cronus castrates his father Ouranos on behalf of his mother Gaia. Cronus himself kills many of the offspring he has with his wife Rhea. Zeus alone is saved through a ruse. These figures have *oedipus complexes*. But does Oedipus?

The esteemed classicist, E. R. Dodds (1970), insists that the warning of the oracle to Oedipus was unconditional. It did not say, as might the biblical prophet "If you do so-and-so, you will kill your father. But if you not do it, you won't." The warning "if X, then Y" implies that "if *not* X, then *not* Y." For example, God sends Jonah to warn the people of Nineveh to change their ways to avoid calamity. They do listen to him and change their outcome, at least temporarily.

The case of Oedipus is very different. This oracle simply pronounces to Oedipus: "You will kill your father; you will sleep with your mother." In other words, the oracle presents Oedipus with the fatalist doctrine, "Y will occur" - and there is nothing Oedipus can do about it. "There is no X that can prevent Y from occurring."

The biblical prophet Nathan is introduced as the defender of Oedipus to provide a Hebrew counterpoint to this view. Nathan's famous encounter with King David after David's role in the death of Uriah, the husband of Bathsheba, indicates the possibility of change and genuine repentance: "Changing X can indeed change Y." David does repent and God ultimately forgives him (2 Samuel 12:1-25).

Nathan lived at about 1000 B.C.E. (see 2 Samuel 7:2-17), but the Great Sanhedrin existed during the Second Temple period (530 B.C.E. to 70 C.E.). Sophocles' play *Oedipus the King* was first performed about 429 B.C.E. though Oedipus himself, if a historical figure, probably lived about 1300 B.C.E. The later biblical prophets Ezra and Nehemiah both returned to Jerusalem after the Babylonian captivity and would have better satisfied the historical chronology. However, the nature and importance of Nathan's encounter with King David led us to juggle the historical chronology and select him as the defender of Oedipus.

The question of whether Dodd's view of the warning of the oracle to Oedipus is prototypical of the Greek view of prophecy bears further discussion. There seem to be exceptions. For example, Apollo gives the Trojan Cassandra the gift of prophecy which seems to give people a choice. If they listen to her, they can escape their doom. However, Apollo's gift to Cassandra is accompanied by the caveat that no one will listen to her, thus taking that choice away. Cassandra's warning to her countrymen not to accept the gift of a Greek horse inside the walls of Troy falls on deaf ears. So even here when the prophetess tries to present people with a choice "if *not* X, then *not* Y," they are programmed not to listen to her, and thus are doomed to their fate: "Y will occur."

Yet Oedipus does try to escape his "fate." He immediately flees Corinth to avoid killing the man he mistakenly thinks is his father (King Polybus) and committing incest with the woman he mistakenly thinks is his mother (Queen Merope). But Oedipus is like Br'er Rabbit in Uncle Remus' tale of *The Tar Baby*. Br'er Fox constructs a lump of tar and puts clothing on it. In this way, Br'er Fox is like the Greek prophet who constructs a false sense of reality for the unwitting Oedipus. When Br'er Rabbit comes along he addresses the "tar baby" amiably, but receives no response. Br'er Rabbit becomes offended by what he perceives as the tar baby's lack of manners, punches it, and becomes stuck. The more he punches, the more stuck he becomes, and he becomes a helpless prey to his arch-enemy Br'er Fox, i.e., like Oedipus falling helpless prey to the false sense of reality constructed for him by the Greek prophet.

However, Br'er Rabbit is able to use his wits to escape Br'er Fox's trap. He tricks Br'er Fox into throwing him into a briar patch, which unknown to Br'er Fox, is a hospitable shelter for Br'er Rabbit. However, Oedipus has no such option in the Greek worldview. Like Br'er Rabbit, the more Oedipus tries to escape his fate, the more deeply trapped in it he becomes. He is stuck in his "tar baby," flailing to no avail. But unlike Br'er Rabbit, Oedipus has no saving "briar patch." Yet, is Oedipus really guilty of anything? Or is Oedipus the prototype of an unwanted and abandoned child, who is saved (physically) by a compassionate shepherd and adopted by another family, but who cannot escape (mentally or emotionally) from the story behind his life that led to his abandonment?

Oedipus in Jerusalem addresses this question in dramatic form.

Kalman J. Kaplan

Characters, Acts and Scenes

CHARACTERS (in order of their appearance)

Oedipus, who kills his father (King Laius) and marries his mother (Queen Jocasta)

Nathan, the biblical prophet

Café waiter

President of the Sanhedrin (Nasi)

Vice president of the Sanhedrin (Av Bet Din)

Sophocles, an ancient Greek tragedian

A guard

Sage 1, a member of the Sanhedrin

Sage 2, a member of the Sanhedrin

Sage 3, a member of the Sanhedrin

Teiresias, a blind prophet of Apollo

Creon, brother of Queen Jocasta and present King of Thebes

Sage 4, a member of the Sanhedrin

Old servant of Laius (King of Thebes)

Old servant of Polybus (King of Corinth)

Messenger (who observed events at the Palace)

Oracle of Delphi (the Pythia)

Spokesman for the Sanhedrin

ACTS AND SCENES

COSTUMES

Oedipus, the Greeks, and the Oracle of Delphi wear Greek clothing. Nathan, the waiter, and members of the Sanhedrin wear Judean attire.

ACT I

Oedipus Wandering:
His Encounter with Nathan

SCENE 1

Dusk in a desolate rocky area near Thebes

A middle-aged man (later revealed to be Oedipus) is seen wandering around a desolate section of wilderness near Thebes. Though he is not that old, he is stooped beyond his years, and dressed in rags. As this solitary figure turns his face to the audience, it realizes he is blind with a slightly blood-stained rag covering his eyes. Yet, despite his desolate condition, he retains a noble but tragic demeanor.

The figure collapses in a heap on the ground, half-sitting and half-lying, swaying from side to side, moaning softly. Beneath his moans, the audience can barely hear him muttering: "No man is born to happiness."

The sky turns black, and night descends.

A second man, Nathan, emerges with the rising sun. He is dressed simply and carrying a staff. He is reciting his morning prayers. As he finishes, he sees the first man (Oedipus) lying on the rocky ground. At first, Nathan is not sure whether Oedipus is alive or dead. Nathan rushes over to Oedipus and sees and hears that he is breathing. Nathan gently lifts up Oedipus' head, and carefully pours water from his jug into Oedipus' mouth. Oedipus slowly awakes, at which point Nathan tenderly washes Oedipus' face and brow. Nathan reaches into his knapsack, takes

*out some milk and honey, and slowly begins to feed Oe-
dipus, making a pillow for him with his knapsack, covering him with his blanket. Oedipus falls back into a more
peaceful sleep.*

*Nathan sees that Oedipus has awakened. He speaks to him
in Aramaic to no response. Then he addresses Oedipus in
Greek, a language that Nathan has some familiarity with
and is Oedipus' native tongue.*

NATHAN: My dear man, how came you to such a wretched state,
alone, famished and blinded?

OEDIPUS (*pointing to the rag around his eyes*): It is far better that
I cannot see.

*Nathan is perplexed. What terrible thing, he wonders has
this man seen that makes him thankful that he is blind.
He waits, expecting Oedipus to say more. But Oedipus has
lapsed into silence.*

NATHAN: My dear man, what has happened that makes you
happy to be blind?

Again, a strange answer on the part of Oedipus.

OEDIPUS: How dreadful is wisdom if it does not benefit the wise?

*Nathan grows more curious by the moment. He looks
more closely at the dried blood on the rag over the eyes
of Oedipus. He gently moves the rag up, and realizes with
horror that Oedipus' eyeballs have been plucked out.*

NATHAN: Who did this to you, most unfortunate man?

*Oedipus is silent, but Nathan does not stop. Nathan asks
again:*

NATHAN: Tell me, who did such a thing to you?

Oedipus again is silent, but Nathan continues. He takes Oedipus by the shoulders, and asks:

NATHAN: Who did this to you, my dear man?

OEDIPUS *(finally responds)*: A better man than I.

NATHAN *(explodes)*: What kind of 'better man' would do such a vile act towards anyone?

OEDIPUS: A man that did not want me to see in the netherworld the people I have wronged.

NATHAN *(exasperated)*: You speak in riddles. Who did this to you, who plucked out your eyeballs? And why do you call such a vile creature a better man than you? Further, why is a man seemingly as noble as yourself, wandering around in the wilderness with no one to care for you? Do you have no family?

OEDIPUS: I did. I had a family, but my sons are gone now. They are all cursed because of me.

NATHAN: My good man, what caused you to lose your family? What terrible event brought you to this state?

OEDIPUS: You don't want to know. What I did so polluted my kingdom of Thebes that it brought a terrible famine to the land.

NATHAN: You speak of Thebes being 'your' kingdom. Does this mean that you were its king?

OEDIPUS: If I were a king, I was a lesser one than my father.

NATHAN: I still do not understand. Was your father king of Thebes?

OEDIPUS: Yes, until he was killed by a knave, leaving my mother as the widowed queen.

NATHAN: What does this have to do with the terrible state you are in? Did you not care for your mother?

OEDIPUS: I cared for her too well. I am tired now and I want to sleep.

Nathan rearranges his knapsack-pillow for Oedipus and covers him again with his blanket. Then Oedipus falls asleep.

SCENE 2

The next morning in the same setting

Oedipus wakes up and finds that Nathan has cooked a small breakfast for him over a fire, along with something warm to drink. During the night, Nathan has wound a clean cloth over Oedipus' eyes. Nathan's mood is softer now, more patient, and less intrusive.

NATHAN: Good morning. How do you feel this morning? You look much more rested, and your color is better.

Oedipus shrugs and nods his assent.

NATHAN: I realize I don't know your name. Who are you?

Oedipus mumbles something hardly audible.

NATHAN: I am Nathan the prophet.

OEDIPUS: Does this mean you know the future?

NATHAN: I don't know the future, but only the effects of one's actions.

OEDIPUS: Then what kind of prophet are you if you cannot prophesy the future?

NATHAN: I am a prophet of the God of Israel.

OEDIPUS: I never heard of such a prophet that does not know the future.

NATHAN: I know how God wishes man to act. What is your name?

OEDIPUS: I am Oedipus, the former King of Thebes.

NATHAN: Why former king?

OEDIPUS: Because the rightful king was killed by a knave.

NATHAN: You have said this yesterday. But how does this make you a former king?

OEDIPUS: Can one who kills a king be a king?

NATHAN: Again you are speaking riddles to me. Speak clearly to me so that I may understand what has happened to you! Where is your wife?

OEDIPUS: Where my mother is.

NATHAN: And where is that, my dear man?

OEDIPUS: Where I will go, and the sooner gone, the better. And, thank Zeus, I will not have to see her.

NATHAN: You will not see her? Who are you referring to, your mother or your wife?

OEDIPUS: When two are one, it is a blessing not to see.

NATHAN: I am very puzzled by you and what has happened to you. How came you to this condition?

OEDIPUS *(sighs)*: Do you really want to hear my story?

NATHAN: Yes, of course I do.

OEDIPUS: I grew up in Corinth, the son of King Polybus and the Queen, the Dorian Merope. One night at a dinner party, I heard talk that I was not the son of those I thought to be my parents.

NATHAN: How did you feel?

OEDIPUS: Confused.

NATHAN: Did you go to your parents to tell them what you had heard?

OEDIPUS: No.

NATHAN: Why not?

OEDIPUS: I was confused. I did not want to insult them. They had been so good to me.

NATHAN: So what did you do?

OEDIPUS: I went to the Oracle of Delphi to find out more.

NATHAN: Who is the Oracle of Delphi?

OEDIPUS: She is Pythia, the priestess of Apollo.

NATHAN: Who is Apollo?

OEDIPUS: The god of the sun.

NATHAN: I don't understand. The sun is not a god. But no matter, what did this oracle say?

OEDIPUS: That I was destined to kill my father and marry my mother.

NATHAN: This is such a strange thing to say. I have never heard of such a thing. In my tradition, one is commanded to honor one's father and mother.

OEDIPUS: But this is what she said.

NATHAN: What did you do?

OEDIPUS I ran away. I did not want to do this to my parents. I immediately fled from Corinth.

NATHAN: To where did you run?

OEDIPUS: To the adjoining kingdom of Thebes.

NATHAN: So what happened then?

Oedipus (visibly tormented) breaks into ironic laughter and then lapses into silence.

SCENE 3

Afternoon in the same setting

NATHAN: Let us continue. So you ran to Thebes to avoid the warning of the oracle.

OEDIPUS: Yes.

NATHAN: So, what happened when you arrived in Thebes?

OEDIPUS: I started traveling on a narrow road and came upon a crossroads where I was blocked by an older man with a group of his assistants. He tried to block my way and I tried to push him aside.

NATHAN: And then what happened?

OEDIPUS: He struck me hard with his staff and fell upon me. I fought him off.

NATHAN: Did you hurt him?

OEDIPUS: I slew him and a number of his assistants in the scuffle. I had not intended to.

NATHAN: What happened next?

OEDIPUS: I went on my way until I arrived at a cliff. At the top of the cliff was a strange creature, a sphinx, with the face of a woman but the body of a lion and with big wings like a huge bird. People were very frightened of it.

NATHAN: I can see its appearance was threatening, but what did this creature do to evoke such fear.

OEDIPUS: It asked passers-by a riddle. If they could not answer the riddle, the creature would swoop down and devour them.

NATHAN: Did this creature present you with a riddle?

OEDIPUS: Yes. But I was able to answer it and thus defeat the creature.

NATHAN: How did the creature respond?

OEDIPUS: The creature killed itself by jumping off of the high cliff. I was brought to the city of Thebes in great honor. As a reward, I was given the queen, who had recently been widowed, as my wife.

NATHAN: So you became King of Thebes?

OEDIPUS: Yes. Yes. Yes.

NATHAN: So you were rewarded for your courageous act.

OEDIPUS: Rewarded? Cursed more than any man ever.

Oedipus stands slowly and walks away. He returns a short while later.

OEDIPUS: I suppose you want me to continue.

NATHAN: Yes. You told me that you had married the Queen of Thebes and became King.

OEDIPUS: Yes.

NATHAN: What happened then?

OEDIPUS: The Queen and I had four children, two sons and two daughters. I ruled as well as I could, I think well . . . until a great plague broke out over the land.

NATHAN: A great plague. What did you do?

OEDIPUS: I was concerned for my subjects, and tried unsuccessfully to end it. But nothing worked. Then Creon, my wife's brother, told me that the plague had been sent due to a "defiling thing which hath been harbored in this land."

NATHAN: So, how did you respond? Did you call in doctors?

OEDIPUS: I asked Creon how Thebes could be cleansed.

NATHAN: What did he say?

OEDIPUS: He said only by banishing a man or killing him in response to bloodshed he had committed which had brought the plague on Thebes.

Oedipus pauses.

OEDIPUS: As I was saying . . .

NATHAN *(smiling):* As you were saying.

OEDIPUS: I did not fully understand what Creon had said. In any city, people murder people, and I myself had defended myself against the man on the road when I first entered Thebes from Corinth. I thought something more must be at stake here. So I questioned Creon more deeply.

NATHAN: What did Creon say? Did he have any answers?

OEDIPUS: Creon said that King Laius of Thebes had been murdered. And that the land of Thebes would not be cleansed until the murderer of Laius would be punished.

NATHAN: How did you answer?

OEDIPUS: I told Creon that I would reopen the investigation immediately. And that I would find the murderer who had polluted the land of Thebes and remove him, not just for Laius, but for myself. For one who kills one king, may kill another.

Nathan shudders.

OEDIPUS: Shall I go on ?

Nathan nods affirmatively.

OEDIPUS: So I started searching for the murderer of King Laius. First, I called in our famed blind seer and prophet Teiresias who knows more than all men. I asked him to shed any light he could on who murdered Laius.

NATHAN: What did this Teiresias say?

OEDIPUS *(groaning)*: He looked very sad, and then spoke in riddles.

NATHAN: What do you mean? What did he say?

OEDIPUS *(shaking)*: He said a thing that seemed so strange to me. "How dreadful is wisdom if it does not benefit the wise."

NATHAN: This is a most strange comment.

OEDIPUS: How I wish I had heeded it.

NATHAN: Go on.

OEDIPUS: I do not want to.

NATHAN: You must.

OEDIPUS: Teiresias did not want to say any more, but I forced him to go on. I threatened him with my power as King of Thebes.

NATHAN: Did he tell you his prophecy?

OEDIPUS: Yes.

NATHAN: What was it?

OEDIPUS: That I myself was the man I was looking for. That I was the polluter of the land of Thebes.

NATHAN: How did you answer?

OEDIPUS: I sent him away in fury, lest I injure this blind old man. I was sick of his damned riddles.

NATHAN: This does reminds me of an event that happened in my own life, when I went to my own King David.

OEDIPUS: Tell me. Why did you go to your king?

NATHAN: Because he had violated the command of The Lord, Our God.

OEDIPUS: What god and what command?

NATHAN: The God of Israel who commanded us not to covet our neighbor's wife.

OEDIPUS: I never have heard of such a god. Is he one of many?

NATHAN: No, He is only One.

OEDIPUS: I never heard of such a thing. One god is not enough.

NATHAN: One God is enough. Many gods are not enough.

OEDIPUS: Now it is you who are speaking in riddles. How can one be more than many?

Nathan smiles and says nothing.

OEDIPUS: What had this David done?

NATHAN: He had coveted and slept with Bathsheba, the wife of Uriah, one of his best soldiers, and then arranged to put Uriah in a position in battle where he was killed. David arranged for Uriah to be killed in battle.

OEDIPUS: Did you approach him with a riddle, as Teiresias did me?

NATHAN: No.

OEDIPUS: How then did you approach him?

NATHAN: In a different way.

OEDIPUS: Had he sent for you?

NATHAN: No.

OEDIPUS: Did he threaten you?

NATHAN: No.

OEDIPUS: Did you tell your king this directly since you did not present him with a riddle?

NATHAN: No.

OEDIPUS: Then how did you tell him?

NATHAN: Through a parable.

OEDIPUS: What is a parable? How did you tell him?

NATHAN: I told him a story of a rich man who had many sheep but, to feed a guest, butchered the only lamb of a poor man.

OEDIPUS: Then what?

NATHAN: I asked my king what he thought should be done with this man.

OEDIPUS: What did your king say?

NATHAN: That the man should be killed.

OEDIPUS: Then what? How did this apply to your king...David?

NATHAN: I looked King David straight in the eye and told him "You are that man."

OEDIPUS And your King David didn't punish you or send you away?

NATHAN: No.

OEDIPUS: What did he do?

NATHAN: He prayed to *HaShem*, our God, and repented of his sin.

OEDIPUS: I don't understand. What do you mean?

NATHAN: That King David admitted his guilt and asked for forgiveness.

OEDIPUS: And?

NATHAN: *HaShem* forgave him over time.

OEDIPUS: You have a very strange king and a very strange god.

NATHAN: No, it is you who have strange gods and oracles. One cannot understand their words. One cannot find meaning or usefulness in them.

SCENE 4

Later that same day in the same setting

Rain falls softly. Nathan has draped a blanket over the two trees by the brook. Nathan and Oedipus sit beneath it.

NATHAN: Can you hear the rain? It is very grey out.

OEDIPUS: Not as grey as I feel.

NATHAN: Please finish your story, as I still cannot put together the pieces of your story.

OEDIPUS: After I sent Teiresias away, I quarreled with Creon for putting him up to this and for accusing me of being the murderer of Laius. I banished him as well. My wife Jocasta heard the quarrel and came down.

NATHAN: Did she make peace between you?

OEDIPUS: She tried. She explained to me that I could not have been the murderer of Laius, because Laius had received a prophecy himself that the infant son of her union with Laius would grow up and kill him. And thus, he ordered a shepherd to leave that infant to die on a mountain top where no one would find him.

NATHAN: So that settled that.

OEDIPUS: Alas, if Jocasta had stopped there, perhaps. But she went on, to ease my fears and tell me that Laius was reported killed by robbers at a place where three roads meet.

NATHAN: Why was this so troubling?

OEDIPUS Because this is where I myself killed an old man who was blocking my path when I first crossed from Corinth to Thebes to avoid the prophecy of killing my father Polybus, King of Corinth.

NATHAN: But you did not kill Polybus.

OEDIPUS: But then another messenger came to the palace just about then to give me the good and bad news that I was to be named King of Corinth as well as Thebes, as my father Polybus had died of the natural cause of old age.

NATHAN: So you did not kill your father. Baruch *HaShem*, blessed be the Name.

OEDIPUS: That is what I thought. But I was still worried that I would marry my mother, Merope. Remember, this was what the Oracle of Delphi had told me.

NATHAN: Yes, I do remember this additional part of the oracle's prophecy.

OEDIPUS: But the messenger laughed and reassured me that this was not a problem, as Polybus was not my natural father, nor Merope my mother. He went on to say that he himself had found me abandoned upon a mountain top when I was just three days old and brought me to his king Polybus who had no son.

NATHAN: So Polybus was not your natural father.

OEDIPUS (*groaning*): No. It was becoming all too clear. I had left Corinth in error.

NATHAN: So what happened next in this story that twists and turns and twists again?

OEDIPUS The attendant who had escaped when Laius was murdered where the three roads crossed came in. He identified me as the murderer. Oh wretched fate. In trying to avoid killing my father, I killed him. In trying to avoid sharing a bed with my mother, I did just that. Laius, and not Polybus, was my father. Jocasta, not Merope, was my mother. And I had entered the same bed in which I was conceived.

NATHAN: But you did not know any of this!

OEDIPUS *(screaming)*: It did not matter. I committed incest!

NATHAN: What did you do next?

OEDIPUS: I rushed in fury to find Jocasta who had betrayed me.

NATHAN *(protesting)*: But she did not know, any more than you did.

OEDIPUS: I rushed to kill her. But I found her already dead, hanging. I took the broach she was wearing and pierced out my eyeballs so I would not have to see her and Laius in the netherworld.

NATHAN: Oh my poor man. Where are your children?

OEDIPUS: My two sons with Jocasta who was mother as well as wife abandoned me. My daughter, Antigone, stayed with me.

NATHAN: Oh my poor man. All this could be avoided. We have had stories of incest in my own people as well, Lot's daughters, and Judah and Tamar, and things turned out very differently. And they knew that they were committing incest, at least the younger of the parties knew.

OEDIPUS Incest is incest. It creates a pollution that must be removed. I am a pollutant, the worst of the worst.

NATHAN: Rest my friend. When you awake, I will take you to a different land, Judea, to be examined by a group of judges, the Sanhedrin, which will look at what happened to you in a different way. This will, perhaps, bring peace to you, my dear, dear man. It seems to me that it is not you but the entire way of thinking of your people that is guilty.

SCENE 5

Boarding a ship to Jaffa

The ship is at stage rear. In the morning, Nathan leads the blind Oedipus on board a ship in the harbor.

OEDIPUS: Where are we going?

NATHAN: To a place to help you put your life back together.

OEDIPUS: It is as impossible for me to put my life together again, as it is to put together an egg, once broken, back whole.

SCENE 6

Morning, three days later in Jaffa

Nathan helps Oedipus disembark.

OEDIPUS Where are we?

NATHAN: We are on land.

OEDIPUS: I know that, but where? Are we in Piraeus?

NATHAN: No, we are in Jaffa.

OEDIPUS Jaffa is not part of Greece.

NATHAN: We are not in Greece.

OEDIPUS: Then where are we?

NATHAN: In Judea.

OEDIPUS: Where is Judea? Is it an island in the Aegean?

NATHAN: No, it is across the Mediterranean.

OEDIPUS: Can you say again the name of where we are?

NATHAN: Jaffa.

OEDIPUS: Jaffa, I have not heard that name. Is it a polis?

NATHAN: No, we do not have polises here.

OEDIPUS: No polises? How do you govern the people?

NATHAN: By following the commandments of God.

OEDIPUS: So, take me to the statue of your god so I can feel how he is formed.

NATHAN: There are no statues of our God.

OEDIPUS: No statues? Why?

NATHAN: We are forbidden to make statues of Him.

OEDIPUS: What nonsense are you saying? We have statues of Zeus.

NATHAN: You do not understand. We do not worship Zeus here.

OEDIPUS: Then take me to your sacred temples where your god is worshiped.

NATHAN: We do not have sacred temples in the sense that you mean.

OEDIPUS: Then take me to your sacred groves.

NATHAN: Neither do we have sacred groves.

OEDIPUS: What kind of god-forsaken place have you brought me to?

NATHAN: To the land of the God of the heavens and of the earth. Now let us find an inn and rest, for you must be weary from the trip. We will talk more later.

SCENE 7

Later that day, in an outside café

Nathan and Oedipus drink tea at the outside café.

NATHAN: Are you feeling better now?

OEDIPUS: Yes, I feel refreshed. But I am very confused.

NATHAN: What is confusing you?

OEDIPUS: Where am I?

NATHAN: As I told you earlier, you are in Judea.

OEDIPUS: I don't know of this "Judea."

NATHAN: We are across the sea from Greece, the Mediterranean Sea.

OEDIPUS: Why did you bring me here?

NATHAN: So you can tell your story to the Sanhedrin.

OEDIPUS: What is the Sanhedrin?

NATHAN: It is our court,

OEDIPUS: Is it like our court in Thebes?

NATHAN: No. it is different.

OEDIPUS: How is it different?

NATHAN: You will see.

A waiter approaches the table.

WAITER: Good afternoon, my friends. Can I offer you something else to eat or drink?

NATHAN: Please bring us some fruit.

OEDIPUS: I don't know the language the man is speaking in. It is not Greek.

NATHAN: It is Aramaic.

OEDIPUS: I don't know this tongue. I am already blind. Do you want to make me deaf as well?

NATHAN: I will be with you. I will be your eyes and your ears.

OEDIPUS *(shouting in anger)*: Why did you bring me here?

NATHAN: So you can tell your story to the Sanhedrin.

OEDIPUS: Again, what is this Sanhedrin?

NATHAN: Our court.

OEDIPUS: How can I tell my story? People do not understand my tongue.

NATHAN: You are wrong. They will. The head of the Sanhedrin is known to speak 70 languages, among which is Greek.

OEDIPUS: I know I am guilty for what I have done. What can this Sanhedrin do?

NATHAN: Wait and see. Now rest and we will continue later in the evening.

SCENE 8

The inn where Nathan and Oedipus are staying

Nathan and Oedipus are sitting at a table in the restaurant. Other guests are speaking loudly in Aramaic or Hebrew.

OEDIPUS: Everyone is speaking so loudly and I can't understand anything.

NATHAN: Do not worry. I am with you.

OEDIPUS: Tell me more about this Sanhedrin. What is it and what does it do?

NATHAN: It is the high court in Judea. It will listen to your story and issue a judgment.

OEDIPUS: Is it a trial?

NATHAN: Yes.

OEDIPUS: But I am guilty of what I have done. Why are you rubbing salt in the wound?

NATHAN: I am not so sure.

OEDIPUS: What are you not sure of?

NATHAN: I am not sure you are guilty.

OEDIPUS: How can this be?

NATHAN: Wait and see.

OEDIPUS: Where is this Sanhedrin? Can we go to it now?

NATHAN: It is not in Jaffa. It is in Jerusalem.

OEDIPUS: What is Jerusalem and where is it?

NATHAN: It is a town some distance from Jaffa where we are now.

OEDIPUS: How will we get there?

NATHAN: We will go by a horse-drawn wagon.

OEDIPUS: When do we go?

NATHAN: I must arrange the trip. Go to rest and I will arrange everything.

SCENE 9

Two days later, Nathan and Oedipus arrive in Jerusalem

OEDIPUS: The wagon has stopped. Where are we?

NATHAN: We have just arrived in Jerusalem.

OEDIPUS: Now what? I don't even know why I am here. I never should have come.

NATHAN: As I told you before, we are going to take you to meet the head of the Sanhedrin. I have written him about your situation.

OEDIPUS: How will he understand me? I don't speak the language of the people here.

NATHAN: My Greek is not so fluent but, as I have said, the head of the Sanhedrin is known to speak 70 languages fluently. Come, he is waiting for us. I have already told him your story.

SCENE 10

Later that day at the office of the Nasi

A guard brings Nathan and Oedipus into the office of the President of the Sanhedrin (Nasi) and leads them to the chairs in front of the Nasi's desk.

NASI *(in fluent Greek)*: Welcome to the Sanhedrin, my friend. I hope you are not too tired from your journey. I am honored that you have come to visit us. I have put some juice and figs before you.

OEDIPUS: I don't know why I am here and why you have agreed to see me.

NASI: Why do you think you are here?

OEDIPUS: I don't know. I don't know why anyone would want to see me after what I have done. I couldn't even bear to see myself nor have my parents see me in the netherworld.

NASI: Is this why you blinded yourself?

OEDIPUS: Wouldn't you have, in my place?

NASI: Let me answer your earlier question. You are here for a number of reasons. First, the prophet Nathan brought you here.

OEDIPUS: Why did you agree to see me?

NASI: Because Nathan told me your story and I was moved by it.

OEDIPUS: Moved by it? I am the most accursed of all men. How could you want to have anything to do with me?

NASI: Let *HaShem* be the judge of that.

OEDIPUS: Who?

NASI: *HaShem*, the name we use to refer to our G-d.

OEDIPUS: Who is *HaShem*?

NASI: *HaShem* is the Creator of the world.

OEDIPUS: Do you mean Earth, *Gaia,* and Sky, *Ouranos*?

NASI: No, I mean the Creator of Heaven, *Shamaim,* and Earth, *Arets.*

OEDIPUS: Do you mean then Fate, *Moira,* and Necessity, *Ananke*?

NASI: I don't understand the question, but no matter. A second reason you have come is because I see how miserable you are and I want to understand more.

NATHAN: I have told the *Nasi* what I have learned from you.

NASI: And I want to see for myself.

Oedipus becomes restless and begins to fidget on his seat.

NATHAN: He paced around much of the night. He was very agitated.

NASI: There is nothing to be agitated about. Let me tell you about the Great Sanhedrin and how your hearing will proceed. The Sanhedrin is a religious assembly of 71 sages who meet in the Chamber of the Hewn Stones in our Temple. This chamber is built in the north wall of the Temple Mount. It is half inside the sanctuary and half outside, with doors providing access to the Temple and the outside. We meet daily during the daytime but do not meet on the Sabbath and festivals.

I am the president, the *Nasi*, and this man sitting next to me is the vice-president, the *Av Bet Din*. Most of the others sit in a semicircle behind us. We judge accused lawbreakers. We require a minimum of two witnesses to convict an accused man. We do not use attorneys. Instead, the accusing witnesses state the offense in the presence of the accused and the accused can call witnesses on his behalf. The court will question the accused, the accusers and the defense witnesses.

OEDIPUS: I have no defense for this worst of all possible actions. I am accursed of the gods. And there is no need for a prosecutor, as I admit I am guilty of everything and see no reason to go on with my life.

NASI: Let us be the judge of this, sir. What will come, will come. In the meantime, I wish to introduce you to a man whom I think you know. He is your countryman, Sophocles the playwright, who has written of your life and accuses you.

OEDIPUS: There is no need for a trial. The gods know how guilty I am.

NASI *(to Sophocles):* Do you intend to accuse Oedipus, esteemed Sophocles?

SOPHOCLES: Yes, I do.

NASI *(to Sophocles):* Do you have a second accuser, Sophocles?

SOPHOCLES: Yes.

NASI *(to Sophocles):* Who is it?

SOPHOCLES: Teiresias the Soothsayer.

NASI *(to Oedipus):* Do you intend to defend yourself, Oedipus?

OEDIPUS *(shouting!):* No! The gods are my witnesses that I am the most guilty and vilest man that ever has lived.

NASI *(continuing on):* Then another man will defend you.

OEDIPUS *(screaming):* Don't you understand? There is nothing to defend. I am the most accursed of all men.

NASI *(continuing):* This man you have come to know well these last few weeks. He is Nathan, the prophet, who has brought you here. Nathan, will you defend Oedipus?

NATHAN Yes, I gladly will, sir.

NASI *(to Nathan):* You will bring in a list of witnesses in your defense of Oedipus?

NATHAN: I can, sir, and I will send it to you before Shabbat.

NASI: There is no need for that. Let us meet again on Sunday when I will receive the list of witnesses from you, Nathan. In the meantime, my friends, please stay calm and enjoy as much as possible the beautiful sunny days and cool nights of Jerusalem. Perhaps, Nathan, you can take Oedipus around the four corners of our beloved city.

END OF ACT 1 AND INTERMISSION

ACT II

Oedipus on Trial

All scenes take place in the courtroom except Scenes 3 and 8. The courtroom should be arranged so that all actors with speaking parts can be seen by the audience. Members of the Sanhedrin who do not speak may be depicted on a backdrop. For example:

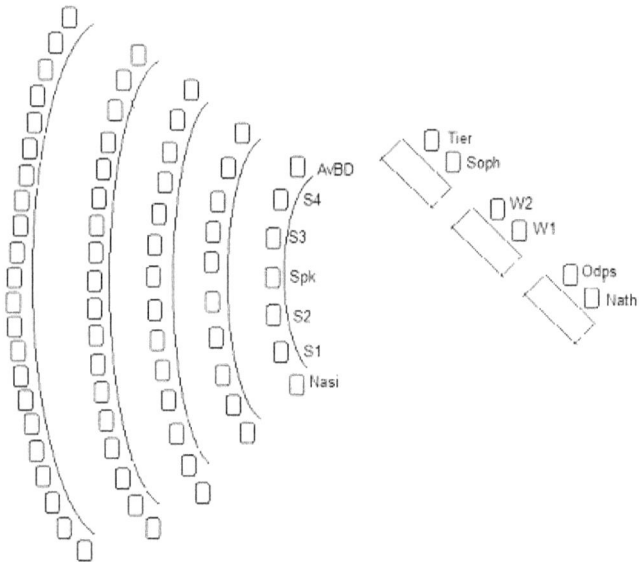

SCENE 1

The trial begins—Nathan announces his witnesses

The president (the Nasi) and the vice-president (the Av Bet Din) are sitting at opposite ends of the first row of a semi-circle of sages (Sage 1, Sage 2, . . . Sage 69). All of them are facing three separate tables, each seating two people, partially facing the audience. Behind the left-hand upper table sit Teiresias and Sophocles; behind the middle table are seats for two witnesses. Behind the right-hand lower table sit Oedipus and Nathan. This arrangement allows the witnesses to answer questions asked by the accusers, the defendant, and members of the Sanhedrin and also to be seen by the audience. Only seven members of the Sanhedrin need be living actors (the Nasi, the Av Bet Din, Sages 1, 2, 3 and 4, and the Spokesman of the Sanhedrin).

A guard leads Oedipus into the Chamber and seats him next to Nathan. In the adjoining room, a number of witnesses are sitting, waiting to be called.

AV BET DIN (*solemnly reading from a papyrus scroll):* The trial of King Oedipus by the Sanhedrin of Jerusalem is now commenced.

NASI: Have you decided on a list of witnesses in your defense of Oedipus?

NATHAN: Yes, I have (*shows the list to the Av Bet Din*).

NASI: Can you read it to us?

NATHAN: Yes. I have composed the following list:

> 1. Creon, the present King of Thebes and brother of the dead Jocasta
>
> 2. The old servant and herdsman who had worked for Laius, the former King of Thebes *(OS Laius)*
>
> 3. The old servant and herdsman who worked for King Polybus of Corinth *(OS Polybus)*
>
> 4. The messenger who observed the events in the palace
>
> 5. The Oracle of Delphi

NASI: Very good. Please remember that any member of the Sanhedrin may ask questions of the accusers, the defendant, and any of the witnesses.

SCENE 2

The accusers, Sophocles and Teiresias, present their case

AV BET DIN *(solemnly reading from a papyrus scroll):* Sophocles, as lead accuser in this case, can you state your charge against Oedipus?

SOPHOCLES: Esteemed council, I charge Oedipus of the crime of purposely killing his father, and subsequently marrying his mother, having sexual relations with her and begetting children with her, as a result causing irreparable damage to his entire family and the community of Thebes at large, as well as offending the gods supporting that community.

AV BET DIN: Can you state your charge more succinctly?

SOPHOCLES: I charge Oedipus with patricide and subsequent incest with his mother.

OEDIPUS *(yelling):* Of course I am guilty!

NATHAN *(attempting to silence him):* I plead that Oedipus is innocent of these charges.

OEDIPUS *(shouting):* Why do you torture me so? I am guilty. Of course I am guilty!

AV BET DIN *(orders a cloth be put in Oedipus' mouth to match the cloth he wears around his gouged-out eyes):* Are there are any questions from any member of the Sanhedrin for the accuser Sophocles?

SAGE 1: Sophocles, can you give us the order of events that leads you to accuse Oedipus of patricide and incest?

SOPHOCLES: I do so gladly. Before Oedipus was born, his father Laius heard from the Oracle at Delphi the prophecy that should Oedipus grow up, he would kill Laius and marry his mother Jocasta.

SAGE 1: My G-d, what did Laius do?

SOPHOCLES: He pierced his son's ankles, thus giving him his name Oedipus or "swollen feet," and then gave the boy to his mother Jocasta to give to their shepherd to be abandoned and left to die.

SAGE 2: But the boy did not die?

SOPHOCLES: No, he was rescued by the shepherd of the adjoining kingdom of Corinth and given to King Polybus to raise.

SAGE 1: Did King Polybus raise him?

SOPHOCLES: Yes, he raised him as his own son.

SAGE 1: So what happened next?

SOPHOCLES: At a certain point, Oedipus heard someone questioning his lineage.

SAGE 2: So what did Oedipus do?

SOPHOCLES: He went to see the Oracle of Delphi.

SAGE 2: What did the oracle tell him?

SOPHOCLES: That he was destined to kill his father and marry his mother.

SAGE 3: What did Oedipus do?

SOPHOCLES: He ran away from Corinth to Thebes.

SAGE 2: So this solved the problem?

SOPHOCLES: Not at all.

SAGE 3: How is that?

SOPHOCLES: Because at a crossroads, Oedipus found his path blocked by his father Laius.

SAGE 1: And?

SOPHOCLES: Oedipus killed him.

SAGE 3: My G-d. What happened next?

SOPHOCLES: Oedipus encountered the Sphinx that was devouring people entering Thebes who could not answer its riddles.

SAGE 2: Did the Sphinx pose a riddle to Oedipus?

SOPHOCLES: Yes.

SAGE 2: Do you know what it was?

SOPHOCLES: I am not certain. I have heard it said that the Sphinx asked him 'Which creature has one voice and yet becomes four-footed and two-footed and three-footed?'

SAGE 2: What did Oedipus answer?

SOPHOCLES: He was reported to have answered 'Man, who crawls on all fours as an infant, walks on two legs as an adult, and with the help of a cane as an elder.'

SAGE 2: But you say you are not certain?

SOPHOCLES: That is correct. For others say the Sphinx posed a different riddle.

SAGE 2: What was that?

SOPHOCLES: 'There are two sisters. One gives birth to the other and she, in turn, gives birth to the first. Who are the two sisters?'

SAGE 2: And how was Oedipus reported to answer this alternate riddle?

SOPHOCLES: 'Day and night, day giving birth to night and then night giving birth to day.'

SAGE 2: Which riddle do you think was posed to Oedipus?

SOPHOCLES: I do not know. I have heard it both ways. What I do know is that Oedipus outwitted the Sphinx by answering whichever riddle was posed.

SAGE 2: And why was this important?

SOPHOCLES: He thereby broke the spell of the Sphinx and its power. This explains why Oedipus was welcomed as a hero in Thebes.

SAGE 3: What was Oedipus' reward for so great a heroic deed?

SOPHOCLES: Oedipus was rewarded by marriage to Jocasta, the widowed Queen of Thebes who was his mother. That is how he became the King of Thebes.

SAGE 3: And is this where things ended?

SOPHOCLES: No, Thebes was experiencing a great plague.

SAGE 3: And?

SOPHOCLES: Oedipus sent his brother-in-law Creon to the Oracle of Delphi to ask what the source of the plague was.

SAGE 3: And what did the oracle answer?

SOPHOCLES: That it was due to the murderer of Laius being in the city and demanded that he be expelled.

SAGE 2: And what happened next?

SOPHOCLES: Oedipus became angry. Ultimately, Jocasta killed herself and Oedipus blinded himself, having learned that he had killed his father and married his mother, bringing all this shame and disaster upon his city.

SAGE 1: Was Oedipus aware of all this?

SOPHOCLES: You will have to ask Oedipus. But his crime is clear. Oedipus killed his father and committed incest with his mother.

NASI: Do you have any more questions?

SAGE 1 (after consulting other sages of the Sanhedrin): No, Adoni.

NASI (to Sophocles): Thank you, Sophocles. You may step down.

AV BET DIN (solemnly reading from a papyrus): Who is the second accuser?

SOPHOCLES: Teiresias, the blind prophet.

AV BET DIN (solemnly reading from a papyrus): Can you state your accusation?

TEIRESIAS: Esteemed council, I too charge Oedipus of the crime of purposely killing his father, and subsequently marrying his mother, having sexual relations with her and begetting children with her, as a result causing irreparable damage to his entire family and the community of Thebes at large, as well as offending the gods supporting that community.

AV BET DIN (to the Sanhedrin): You may ask Teiresias questions now.

SAGE 1: When did you meet Oedipus?

TEIRESIAS: When Creon, the brother-in-law of Oedipus, brought me to him.

SAGE 2: Can you tell us what transpired?

TEIRESIAS: Oedipus told me that Phoebus Apollo had sent the people of Thebes an answer to their question regarding how to cure the pestilence that was afflicting them. The cure was to find the men who murdered Laius and kill them or expel them from the land as exiles. That would save the people of Thebes by delivering them from the pollution caused by this crime.

SAGE 2: How did you respond?

TEIRESIAS: That I wanted to leave and return home. That it is dreadful to have wisdom that brings no benefit to the person possessing it.

SAGE 3: That was a strange answer. Why did you answer that way?

TEIRESIAS: Because I did not want to cause Oedipus distress.

SAGE 3: How did Oedipus respond?

TEIRESIAS: Badly. He said that my response revealed little love and he implored me to use my prophetic voice to help the city that nurtured me. I said that I did not want to say what was inside of me.

SAGE 2: Why not?

TEIRESIAS: Because my words would only distress him.

SAGE 3: I don't understand. Are you not a seer and a prophet?

TEIRESIAS: So people say about me.

SAGE 3: So could you not have used your gift of prophecy to help Oedipus fix the problem in Thebes?

TEIRESIAS: No.

SAGE 1: Why not?

TEIRESIAS: Because I only can see the future, I cannot change it.

SAGE 1: This is a very strange definition of prophecy. Do you mean that nothing you could have said to Oedipus could have helped him change the situation?

TEIRESIAS: No, it was all fated. Everything is determined by fate, *moira*, and necessity, *ananke*. He was fated to kill his father and marry his mother.

SAGE 2: Did King Oedipus accept your words and let you leave?

TEIRESIAS: Absolutely not, he did the opposite. He became irate and asked me if I intended to betray him and destroy Thebes.

SAGE 2: And?

TEIRESIAS: I insisted that I had no wish to cause him or myself distress, and asked him why he continued to fruitlessly question me.

SAGE 2: And then?

TEIRESIAS: He accused me of being most disgraceful with possessing an unending stubbornness. I maintained my silence until Oedipus accused me of conspiring in the murder of Laius myself, short of actually doing the killing, because of blindness.

SAGE 2: How did you respond to this accusation?

TEIRESIAS: I lost my temper and could not hold my words in. I accused Oedipus himself of being the accursed polluter of the land.

SAGE 2: How did he respond to your accusation?

TEIRESIAS: He became angry, He accused me of telling a disgraceful lie, which I would regret. I responded I had not wanted to speak but that he had incited me to do so. But then he did not seem to grasp the meaning of what I was saying, asking me to repeat myself. I told him again that he himself was the man he was looking for. He then turned his fury on me.

SAGE 2: What did Oedipus say then?

TEIRESIAS: He told me that truth was not in me, that my ears and mind were as blind as my eyes are. If this insult was not enough, he then accused me of conspiring with Creon to overthrow him and install Creon as king in his place.

SAGE 2: And how did you respond?

TEIRESIAS: I denied this, saying Creon was no threat and that Oedipus himself had caused this trouble on his own.

SAGE 2: What did Oedipus say?

TEIRESIAS: He said that with all my prophecy, I had not solved the riddle of the Sphinx that was terrorizing travelers to Thebes. But that he, Oedipus, with his wits was able to pierce the secret to the Sphinx' riddle, and thus free Thebes from its torment. That my conspiracy with Creon would not succeed in usurping the state, and that we would regret our action. And that if I did not look so old, I would find the punishment my arrogance deserved.

SAGE 2: What did you say?

TEIRESIAS: I answered forthrightly that I was not his slave. That I served Apollo and thus would never stand with Creon or sign on as his man. And that though he had chosen to insult my blindness – even though he had his eyesight, he did not see how miserable he was, or where he lived, or who it was who shared his household.

SAGE 2: And?

TEIRESIAS: I asked the boy who brought me to lead me away. Oedipus concurred, telling me that I was in the way if I stayed and would just provoke him further.

SAGE 2: Did you leave?

TEIRESIAS: I did, but I could not withhold my final comment to him. I told him why I had come, that the man he was seeking who murdered Laius was living in Thebes, that he will be poor though now he was rich, and would grope the ground before him with a stick. And he will turn out to be the brother of the children in his house – their father, too, both at once, and the husband and the son of the very woman who gave birth to him. That he sowed the same womb as his father and murdered him. I then left, and have encountered Oedipus again only now.

SAGE 2: Thank you, my esteemed Teiresias. That is all I have to ask.

AV BET DIN (solemnly reading from a list): Are there any other accusers?

SOPHOCLES: No.

AV BET DIN: Then let the defense begin its case and present witnesses. Who is the defendant?

OEDIPUS (shouting): I have nothing to defend. I am the most guilty of all people. I killed my father and married my mother.

AV BET DIN: As I said before, I will appoint Nathan the Prophet to represent Oedipus. Are you willing to do this, Nathan?

NATHAN: Yes, I am.

AV BET DIN: How do you plead?

NATHAN (over Oedipus' shouted objections): I plead that Oedipus is innocent of the charges. That he did all in his power to avoid killing his father and marrying his mother, but was entrapped by maddening riddles, incomplete information and confused identities.

AV BET DIN: We will adjourn until tomorrow.

SCENE 3

Nathan encounters Teiresias at a café later that day

The blind Teiresias is seated in a café drinking a bottle of wine when Nathan, by chance, enters the café. Looking around the room, Nathan recognizes Teiresias. He comes over to him and speaks to him in Greek.

NATHAN: My esteemed Teiresias, may I join you?

TEIRESIAS: Who is this? Who are you?

NATHAN: Nathan, the prophet.

TEIRESIAS: Have we met?

NATHAN: No. I am representing Oedipus in the trial.

TEIRESIAS: Yes, now I recognize your voice. Please sit down.

Nathan sits down. The waiter comes to the table.

WAITER *(to Nathan)*: Would you like to drink something?

NATHAN: Yes.

WAITER: Good. What would you like?

NATHAN: I would like a bottle of wine.

The waiter brings a bottle of wine. Nathan pours some into a glass and begins to drink.

NATHAN *(to Teiresias)*: I was very interested in what you said in the courtroom.

TEIRESIAS: About what?

NATHAN: About prophecy.

TEIRESIAS: What about "prophecy"?

NATHAN: That you knew the future.

TEIRESIAS: That is sometimes a curse rather than a blessing.

NATHAN: But that you could not change the future.

TEIRESIAS: You are correct. That is what makes such knowledge a curse.

NATHAN: But could you not warn others about what you have seen?

TEIRESIAS: Yes, but they would hate me for it.

NATHAN: But could you not warn people of impending doom?

TEIRESIAS: Again, they would hate me for it.

NATHAN: But could they then not change their ways to avoid their doom?

TEIRESIAS: The future cannot be changed.

NATHAN: Then what good is prophecy?

TEIRESIAS: Exactly. It can be, as I say, a curse.

SCENE 4

The 1st defense witness—Creon, brother of Queen Jocasta

NASI: Are you ready to call the witnesses you have given us?

NATHAN: Yes, Adoni.

NASI: Who is your first witness?

NATHAN: Creon, the brother of the dead Queen Jocasta and now the King of Thebes.

> *The first defense witness, King Creon of Thebes, is brought in.*

NATHAN: Please identify yourself.

CREON: I am Creon, King of Thebes.

NATHAN: Do you know the defendant *(gestures towards Oedipus)*.

CREON: Yes, he was the husband of my dear departed sister, Jocasta.

NATHAN: Do you know what Oedipus is charged with?

CREON: I do.

NATHAN: Can you give us any information about the matter?

CREON: Thebes was suffering under a plague, and Oedipus, then King after the death of Laius, sent me to Apollo's shrine to learn from him what we might do or say to save our city.

NATHAN: Did you learn anything of use?

CREON: Yes, I heard from the god that Lord Phoebus clearly ordered us to drive away the polluting stain this land had harbored – which would not be healed if we kept nursing it.

NATHAN: Did you report this to Oedipus?

CREON: I did, I reported this to Oedipus who urged me to speak out to everyone.

NATHAN: Did you do this publicly?

CREON: Yes. Oedipus urged me to speak out in front of to everyone.

Oedipus begins to shout and is gagged.

NATHAN: And did Oedipus respond?

CREON: He did. He asked me what sort of cleansing? And he asked how this disaster happened.

NATHAN: What did you answer?

CREON: By banishment, I said, or by shedding blood again to atone for the murder. I went on to explain that before he, Oedipus, came to steer our ship of state, Laius ruled this land and that he had been murdered. And now the god is clear: those murderers, he tells us, must be punished, whoever they may be.

NATHAN: Did Oedipus seem to know anything about this?

CREON: Not that I could tell.

NATHAN: Did Oedipus pursue the matter further?

CREON: He asked in what country these murderers lived, and worried if they would be hard to track.

NATHAN: What did you say?

CREON: I answered that they were in Thebes itself. He asked whether Laius fell in Thebes, and I responded that he died abroad, on his way to Delphi, and never returned.

NATHAN: Did Oedipus ask anything else?

CREON: He asked if there were any witnesses to the event. I responded there was only one who ran away, who reported that Laius had been killed by a gang of men, not just one. Oedipus then asked what had kept us from investigating the crime.

NATHAN: How did you respond?

CREON: I said we had been distracted by the Sphinx who was threatening all who wanted to enter Thebes with her enigmatic riddles, and devouring all who could not answer them. This had forced us to concentrate on addressing that urgent problem and to put aside the investigation of the death of Laius.

NATHAN: What did Oedipus say?

CREON: That he would reopen the investigation and shed light on darkness. That he would remove the polluting stain from the land. I suggested that he consult Teiresias, the Prophet, and we parted company.

NATHAN: Did you meet with Oedipus again after that?

CREON: I did.

NATHAN: Was this meeting similar or different from your previous meeting?

CREON: It was completely different.

NATHAN: How so?

CREON: Oedipus immediately accused me of being the murderer of Laius and also of wanting to steal Oedipus' throne. He asked me if I planned to do such a thing because I thought he was a coward or a fool. He then asked, "Or did you think I would not learn about your actions as they crept up on me with such deceit – or that I could not deflect them?"

NATHAN: What was your answer?

CREON: I asked him to listen to me and let me make a suitable response so he could judge for himself. However he refused to listen, calling me a trouble-maker and accusing me of betraying him. I told him he was being stubborn and forgetting common sense. He told me I was not thinking clearly if I thought that I could injure him and escape penalty. I agreed and asked him what damage I had done him.

NATHAN: What did he say?

CREON: He began by asking me, "Did you not persuade me to send for Teiresias, that prophet?". I responded that I had and I would give him still the same advice. King Oedipus then digressed and asked me how long ago King Laius was brutally killed.

NATHAN: How did you answer?

CREON: That it had happened many years ago. Oedipus then asked me if Teiresias then was skilled in prophecy at that time. I answered that he was then as he is at the present time.

NATHAN: Where do you think Oedipus' questioning was leading?

CREON: He asked if back at the time of the killing of Laius, had Teiresias ever mentioned him (*points to Oedipus*). I answered that Teiresias had never done so in my presence. Oedipus asked me if I had not investigated the killing. I said we did but we found nothing. Again he asked why Teiresias has not spoken up at the time. I said I did not know.

NATHAN: So the matter then came to rest?

CREON: No, he accused me again of working with Teiresias, and this being the motive of Teiresias for naming him as the one who murdered Laius. I said to Oedipus that I did not know what Teiresias had told him. But then I added that the time had come for me to question him.

NATHAN: How did he respond?

CREON: He said I could ask all I want, but that I would not be able to prove that he was the murderer of Laius. I asked him, first, if he was not married to my sister Jocasta. He admitted this. I asked him if the two of them did not rule Thebes as equals. He answered that whatever she desires, she receives from him. I asked him, if I was not third, equal to them both. Oedipus responded that this is what has made my actions so deceitful.

NATHAN: How did you reply?

CREON: That I already had the powers I wanted and would rather live in peace—carefree and safe—unburdened by the yoke of kingship and the anxiety attendant to that responsibility. I continued, stating that if he wanted proof of my innocence, to go to Delphi and ask the Oracle if I had accurately transmitted his words to Oedipus. "If you discover that I had planned something with Teiresias," I said, "then arrest me and have me put to death not just on his own authority, but on mine as well, a double judgment." I added that, in my view, to throw away a noble friend is like a man who parts with his own life, the thing most dear to him. I suggested that if he would give it some time, he would see clearly, since only time can fully validate a man who is true. A bad man is exposed in just one day.

NATHAN: How did Oedipus respond to your eloquent words? Did they change his mood and his mind?

CREON: Alas, no. He said if some conspirator moves against him, in secret and with speed, he must be quick to make his counter plans, stating that if he just rests and waits for the conspirator to act, then the conspirator will succeed in what he seeks to do, and that he, Oedipus, would be finished. I asked if he wanted to exile me from Thebes. He responded, no, that he wanted me to die, not just run off, so that he could demonstrate what envy brings.

NATHAN: Did you try to change his mind?

CREON: I did, but he said I would not convince him for there was no way he could trust me.

NATHAN: Yet, I can see you are still very much alive. So some force must have intervened.

CREON: My sister Jocasta arrived in the palace and heard our quarrel. I told her that her husband Oedipus intended to either banish me from my fathers' country or arrest me and then have me killed. Oedipus responded that I was correct and that he had caught me committing treason, conspiring against his royal authority.

NATHAN: What happened then?

CREON: I swore that I had not done what he had accused me of. Jocasta implored him to trust me, and respect the oath I had made before all heaven, for her sake, and for those around me. People around also implored him to not punish me so.

NATHAN: How did Oedipus respond?

CREON: He agreed to let me go, then, even though it was clear that he himself would be killed or sent from Thebes in exile, forced out in disgrace. He added that he had been moved to act compassionately by what Jocasta had said, not by my words. But he added that if I stayed in Thebes, I would be hateful to him.

NATHAN: What did you say?

CREON: I responded that he was obstinate, unhappy to concede, and unable to tolerate himself. He told me to go and leave him alone. I responded that I would leave as he did not understand me even though people in Thebes knew that I was a reasonable man.

NATHAN: Did you leave?

CREON: Yes, for a while.

NATHAN *(to Nasi)*: I am finished questioning this witness.

NASI: Are there any questions from the judges?

SAGE 1: Would you describe Oedipus as a good or bad king before these terrible events unfolded?

CREON: A good, conscientious king.

SAGE 2: Would you describe Oedipus as a good or bad husband prior to these terrible events?

CREON: A good, loving husband.

SAGE 3: Would you describe Oedipus as a good or bad father prior to these terrible events?

CREON: A good, loving father.

SAGE 4: You have told the court about the plague that fell upon Thebes. Have you anything to add to this?

CREON: Nothing.

SAGE 4: You testified you learned from the Oracle at Apollo's shrine that the plague would not be healed unless a polluting stain was driven from the land.

CREON: Yes.

SAGE 1: How did Oedipus react?

CREON: In a very concerned manner. He urged me to speak out to everyone.

SAGE 1: You testified earlier that he asked what caused this plague.

CREON: Yes.

SAGE 2: You testified earlier that that the plague was due to the murder of Laius, the previous King of Thebes.

CREON: Yes.

SAGE 2: Did Oedipus seem to know anything about this?

CREON: He did not, but said we should shed light on the darkness and that he would remove the polluting stain from the land. As I testified before, I suggested that he speak with the blind Teiresias.

SAGE 2: What happened then?

CREON: He did speak to Teiresias.

SAGE 3: You testified before that your relationship with Oedipus changed radically.

CREON: Yes, after his meeting with Teiresias, he accused me of being myself the murderer of Laius and conspiring with Teiresias to try to steal his throne. And that I would not be able to prove that he was the murderer of Laius.

SAGE 3: How did you respond?

CREON: As I said before, I was stunned, as I always had been loyal to Oedipus. I told him so.

SAGE 4: Had you ever thought he might be the murderer of Laius?

CREON: No.

SAGE 4: Did he indicate that he thought he might be the murderer?

CREON: No.

NASI: Are there any more questions for this witness from anyone in our Sanhedrin?

No response from any member of the Sanhedrin.

NASI: In that case, you may step down. *(to Nathan):* You may call the next witness.

SCENE 5

The 2nd and 3rd defense witnesses—Old servants of King Laius and King Polybus

Oedipus is ungagged. The second defense witness, the old servant of Laius, is brought in.

NATHAN: Can you please identify yourself?

OLD SERVANT OF LAIUS: I am a shepherd.

NATHAN: Some time ago did you work for King Laius of Thebes?

OLD SERVANT OF LAIUS: Yes, as a slave. But I was not bought. I grew up in his house.

NATHAN: How did you live? What was the work you did?

OLD SERVANT OF LAIUS: As I said before, I am a shepherd. I have spent most of my life looking after sheep.

NATHAN: Where? In what particular areas?

OLD SERVANT OF LAIUS: On Cithaeron or the neighboring lands.

NATHAN: Do you recall this man seated here (*pointing to Oedipus*)?

OLD SERVANT OF LAIUS: Yes I do. He was born in Laius' house.

NATHAN: From a slave or from some relative of his?

OLD SERVANT OF LAIUS: I was told the child was his. Laius' wife gave the child to me.

NATHAN: Why did she do that?

OLD SERVANT OF LAIUS: So I would expose him on the mountain and leave him to die.

NATHAN: Why would she do something like that?

OLD SERVANT OF LAIUS: She was afraid of dreadful prophecies.

NATHAN: What sort of prophecies?

OLD SERVANT OF LAIUS: That the boy would kill his father and marry his mother.

NATHAN: If that were true, how is it you did not kill the child?

OEDIPUS (screaming): How I wish you had!

OLD SERVANT OF LAIUS: I pitied the boy, master, and I gave him to another shepherd in the next field with the thought that he would take the child off to a foreign land.

NATHAN: Have you seen this shepherd again?

OLD SERVANT OF LAIUS: Not for many years. Not until now.

NATHAN: Until now?

OLD SERVANT OF LAIUS: He is sitting in this court room now.

NATHAN: Can you identify him?

> The old servant of Laius points to the old servant of Polybus.

NATHAN *(to the Nasi):* May I call the old servant of Polybus as my third witness and then recall the old servant of Laius?

NASI: You may.

NATHAN *(to the Nasi):* Might I ask that the esteemed Sanhedrin withhold from asking questions of either witness until I finish?

NASI: The members of the Sanhedrin are so instructed.

The third defense witness, the old servant of Polybus, is brought in.

NATHAN: Good morning, sir. Can you please identify yourself?

OLD SERVANT OF POLYBUS: I am a shepherd. I have been the servant of King Polybus of Corinth.

NATHAN: I understand you came to present news to King Oedipus of Thebes.

OLD SERVANT OF POLYBUS: I came to tell him the sad news of King Polybus' death of old age and also the good news that the people who lived there, in the lands beside the Isthmus, had announced that they would make Oedipus their king.

NATHAN: So King Polybus died a natural death?

OLD SERVANT OF POLYBUS: Yes, of old age.

NATHAN: And Oedipus did not kill him?

OLD SERVANT OF POLYBUS: No, of course not. Oedipus seemed to be very relieved that he was not responsible for the death of his father. For fear of killing him, Oedipus had left Corinth. I responded that he had worried needlessly as King Polybus was not his natural father.

NATHAN: So all was resolved at this stage?

OLD SERVANT OF POLYBUS: No, Oedipus became agitated and said that he wanted to meet with an old servant of Laius, King of Thebes.

NATHAN: Was Queen Jocasta there?

OLD SERVANT OF POLYBUS: Yes

NATHAN: What was her response?

OLD SERVANT OF POLYBUS: She was very distressed. She did not want him to meet the servant. She implored him to stop, telling him she cared about his own wellbeing.

NATHAN: Did Oedipus listen to her?

OLD SERVANT OF POLYBUS: No, he did not. He told her that her words brought him more distress and ordered that the shepherd be brought to him.

NATHAN: What was Jocasta's response?

OLD SERVANT OF POLYBUS: I remember her words. She called Oedipus a miserable man who would not listen to her and told him she would never speak again. And she ran into the palace.

NATHAN: What happened next?

OLD SERVANT OF POLYBUS: The old servant of King Laius arrived.

NATHAN: And what happened?

OLD SERVANT OF POLYBUS: Oedipus began questioning him.

NATHAN: What did Oedipus ask him?

OLD SERVANT OF POLYBUS: If he had been a herdsman of King Laius.

NATHAN: And?

OLD SERVANT OF POLYBUS: He said he had. Oedipus asked him "Where?"

NATHAN: So where?

OLD SERVANT OF POLYBUS: Somewhere near Cithaeron. Oedipus then asked him if he had met me before?

NATHAN: What did he say?

OLD SERVANT OF POLYBUS: That he could not remember.

NATHAN: And then?

OLD SERVANT OF POLYBUS: I refreshed his memory of how he herded flocks in the adjoining fields in the region of Cithaeron.

NATHAN: And?

OLD SERVANT OF POLYBUS. I asked the old man if he remembered giving me an infant boy to be raised as my own foster son.

NATHAN: What did he say?

OLD SERVANT OF POLYBUS: He said nothing. However, Oedipus demanded he go on.

Oedipus begins to howl. Nathan ignores Oedipus.

NATHAN: Did he go on?

OLD SERVANT OF POLYBUS: Yes. He was forced to. Oedipus asked him if he had indeed given me the infant.

NATHAN: What did the old man say?

OLD SERVANT OF POLYBUS: He admitted he had. Oedipus asked if the child was his.

NATHAN: What did the servant of Laius say?

OLD SERVANT OF POLYBUS: He answered that the child was from the house of Laius. And that Queen Jocasta had given him the child.

NATHAN: How did Oedipus respond?

OLD SERVANT OF POLYBUS: He asked why this occurred? Why did she give him the infant?

NATHAN: What did he answer?

OLD SERVANT OF POLYBUS: To kill it. Oedipus of course asked "Why?".

NATHAN: What did the Servant of Laius answer?

OLD SERVANT OF POLYBUS: Because of her fear of an evil prophesy that the infant, when grown, would kill his father.

OLD SERVANT OF POLYBUS: Oedipus looked like he was hit by lightning, muttering that it all came true and was now clear. Then he said something to the effect that he was cursed by birth and by his own family, and by a murder he should not have committed.

NATHAN: And then?

OLD SERVANT OF POLYBUS: He ran into the palace, shouting "Light, let me look at you one final time."

NATHAN: Did Oedipus stay in the palace? And what of Jocasta?

OLD SERVANT OF POLYBUS: A messenger came running out screaming that he had seen the vilest things.

NATHAN: Is the messenger in the courtroom?

OLD SERVANT OF POLYBUS: Yes, he is (*pointing to a man sitting quietly in the courtroom*).

NATHAN: Thank you, sir; you may step down now.

NATHAN *(to the Nasi):* I wish to recall now my second witness, the old servant of Laius.

The second witness (the old servant of Laius) returns and sits in the witness chair.

NATHAN *(to the old servant of Laius):* Thank you for coming back. I want to clear something up. Who was the father of Oedipus?

OLD SERVANT OF LAIUS: Laius, King of Thebes.

NATHAN: Did Laius die a natural death?

OLD SERVANT OF LAIUS: No, he was murdered.

NATHAN: How do you know this?

OLD SERVANT OF LAIUS *(uncomfortably):* I was there.

NATHAN: So you witnessed it?

OLD SERVANT OF LAIUS *(more uncomfortably):* Yes, I witnessed it.

NATHAN: Can you tell us what happened?

OLD SERVANT OF LAIUS: We, five of us, were traveling in a horse-drawn carriage in a spot where three roads meet. At that place we met a man coming toward us who was blocking our path. When our driver tried to drive our carriage through, the man in a rage lashed out at him. When King Laius hit him, the man retaliated by hitting Laius with a blow from the staff he held and knocked him from the carriage to the road, leaving him lying on his back. Then this man killed everyone else in our party. I alone was able to escape.

NATHAN: Can you identify this man?

OLD SERVANT OF LAIUS (reluctantly): Yes, I can. This is the man (pointing to the now gagged Oedipus who is desperately trying to speak from beneath his gag).

The court erupts.

NATHAN: Did the two men seem to know each other?

OLD SERVANT OF LAIUS: No, they did not.

NATHAN: Then why was Laius killed?

OLD SERVANT OF LAIUS: As I said before, over a quarrel as to who would cross the intersection first.

NATHAN: I want to ask you again. Did King Laius and this man (*pointing to Oedipus*) seem to know each other?

OLD SERVANT OF LAIUS: No, they did not.

NATHAN: Thank you. You may step down. I wish to recall the third witness, the old servant of King Polybus.

> *Oedipus is sitting gagged. The third witness (the old servant of Polybus) returns and is sworn in.*

NATHAN (*to the old servant of Polybus*): Good morning again, sir. Please tell us once again who you are.

OLD SERVANT OF POLYBUS: As I said before, I have been the servant of King Polybus of Corinth.

NATHAN: You testified that you came to present news to King Oedipus of Thebes of the death of Polybus.

OLD SERVANT OF POLYBUS: Yes

NATHAN: And King Polybus died a natural death?

OLD SERVANT OF POLYBUS: Yes, of old age.

NATHAN: And Oedipus did not kill him?

OLD SERVANT OF POLYBUS: No, of course not.

NATHAN: But Polybus was not the father of Oedipus?

OLD SERVANT OF POLYBUS: No, he was not. He was his adoptive father. I brought the abandoned Oedipus as an infant to Polybus to raise as his own.

NATHAN: Did Oedipus know that Polybus was not his father?

OLD SERVANT OF POLYBUS: No, I do not think so.

NATHAN: Why do you say this?

OLD SERVANT OF POLYBUS: Because it was rumored that Oedipus went to an oracle who told him he was destined to kill his father.

NATHAN: What was the result of this?

OLD SERVANT OF POLYBUS: Oedipus left Corinth to avoid any chance of fulfilling this prophecy.

NATHAN: So Oedipus thought Polybus was his biological father.

OLD SERVANT OF POLYBUS: I think this is clear. Oedipus left Corinth to avoid any chance of fulfilling the prophecy that he would kill his father whom he thought was King Polybus.

NATHAN: Thank you.

NATHAN *(to the Nasi and the Av Bet Din):* I am finished questioning these two witnesses.

NASI: These two witnesses are open for questioning by members of the Sanhedrin.

SAGE 1 *(to the old servant of Laius)*: Did you feel any hesitation in exposing Oedipus to die?

OLD SERVANT OF LAIUS: Yes I did. This is why I gave him to the shepherd of King Polybus.

SAGE 1 *(to the old servant of Laius):* Were you not afraid that King Laius would punish you for not carrying out his orders.

OLD SERVANT OF LAIUS: Yes, I was afraid.

SAGE 1 *(to the old servant of Laius):* So you never told them that you had not left Oedipus to die?

OLD SERVANT OF LAIUS: Of course not.

SAGE 2 *(to the old servant of Laius):* So Laius and Jocasta thought that Oedipus was dead.

OLD SERVANT OF LAIUS: They would not have had cause to think otherwise.

SAGE 3 *(to the old servant of Polybus):* Did Oedipus know that his father Laius had tried to kill him?

OLD SERVANT OF POLYBUS: No. He did not even know Laius was his father. He thought Polybus was his father.

SAGE 2 *(to the old servant of Polybus):* So Queen Jocasta did not know Oedipus was her son?

OLD SERVANT OF POLYBUS: No. She thought that her son was dead.

SAGE 3 *(to the old servant of Laius):* Did Laius recognize Oedipus on the road?

OLD SERVANT OF LAIUS: No, he did not.

SAGE 4 *(to the old servant of Laius):* Did Oedipus seem to recognize Laius on the road.

OLD SERVANT OF LAIUS: No, he did not. Not that I could tell.

SAGE 1 *(to the old servant of Polybus):* Why did Oedipus leave the Kingdom of Corinth, given that he would be king some day?

OLD SERVANT OF POLYBUS: I thought it was very strange at the time and none of us understood why he did it.

SAGE 1 *(to the old servant of Polybus)*: Do you now understand his behavior?

OLD SERVANT OF POLYBUS: Yes, he thought he would hurt Polybus and fled to avoid doing so.

SAGE 1 *(to the old servant of Polybus)*: But his fleeing was unnecessary?

OLD SERVANT OF POLYBUS: Yes.

SAGE 2 *(to the old servant of Polybus)*: Could you tell us why again?

OLD SERVANT OF POLYBUS: Because Polybus was not his natural father.

NASI: If there are no more questions for these two witnesses, we will proceed to the next witness. *(to Nathan)*: Can we move to your next witness for the defense?

NATHAN: Yes. I would like to call the messenger who witnessed the events inside the palace.

SCENE 6

The 4th defense witness—
The messenger

The messenger who witnessed the events inside the Palace is seated.

NATHAN: Can you please identify yourself?

MESSENGER: I am a messenger in the royal palace of Thebes.

NATHAN: Sir, did you witness an event inside the Palace?

MESSENGER: Yes I did.

NATHAN: What did you see?

MESSENGER: First, that Jocasta had run into the palace, frantic, straight to her marriage bed, crying out to her dead husband Laius that the child of theirs, conceived so many years ago, had killed her husband who had left her to conceive cursed children with that child. She lay moaning in her bed, where she had given birth twice over, a husband from a husband, children from a child.

NATHAN: My God. What happened then?

MESSENGER: Oedipus came charging in, asking us to give him a sword, as he tried to find her.

NATHAN: Did he find her?

MESSENGER: Yes, later, hanging by the neck, swaying, with twisted cords wrapped around her neck. We followed Oedipus as he raced in, as if pushed by someone. He leapt at the double doors, bent the bolts out of their sockets by force, and burst into her room.

NATHAN: That's where he found her?

MESSENGER: Yes, we all saw Jocasta, hanging there, swaying, with twisted cords wrapped round her neck. When Oedipus saw her, he took her body out of the noose in which she hung, and then, when the poor woman was lying on the ground, he ripped off the golden brooches she wore as ornaments, raised them high, and drove them deep into his own eyeballs, crying as he did so: "You will no longer see all those atrocious things I suffered, the dreadful things I did! No. You have seen those you never should have looked upon and those I wished to know you did not see. So now and for all future time, be dark!" With these words, Oedipus raised his hands and struck, not once, but many times, right at his eye sockets. With every blow blood spurted from his eye sockets down on his beard, not in single drops but showers of dark blood spattered like hail.

NATHAN: What did you witness next?

MESSENGER: Oedipus came out through the palace door, blood flowing from his eyes, an appalling sight, speaking of his endless shame, shouting that he had been abandoned by the gods, the son of a corrupted mother, conceiving children with the woman who gave him his own miserable life.

NATHAN: Did people just leave him?

MESSENGER: No, Creon, now the only guardian of Thebes, took pity on him, took Oedipus inside, and brought his children to him.

NATHAN: And?

MESSENGER: Oedipus asked Creon to send him away to live outside of Thebes. However, Creon responded that only the gods could give him what he asked.

NATHAN: How did Oedipus respond?

MESSENGER: He said that he had become abhorrent to the gods. Creon said that then he should quickly get what he desired but that he should still trust the gods. They seemed to agree that Oedipus would live outside of Thebes.

NATHAN *(to the Nasi)*: I am finished asking this witness questions.

NASI *(to the Sanhedrin which is sitting in stunned silence)*: Do you have any questions for this witness?

SAGE 1 *(to the messenger)*: What you witnessed is so terrible. It seems clear that Oedipus at this point realized what he had done.

MESSENGER: Yes.

SAGE 2 *(to the messenger)*: And Jocasta also?

MESSENGER: Yes.

SAGE 3 *(to the messenger)*: Do you think this is the first time they realized it?

MESSENGER: It seems so.

SAGE 4 *(to the messenger)*: Do you think they knew what they had done before this?

MESSENGER: I think that this is the first time they realized it.

NASI *(to the Sages who are still sitting stunned)*: Do you have any more questions for this witness?

The Sages make no response.

NASI *(to Nathan)*: In that case, let us hear your last witness, the Oracle of Delphi.

SCENE 7

The 5th defense witness— The Oracle of Delphi

An unkempt middle-aged woman with long hair comes to the witness stand. She appears to be hallucinatory and speaks in a strange depersonalized voice.

NATHAN: Can you please identify yourself?

ORACLE OF DELPHI: Says something inaudible.

NATHAN: Are you the Oracle of Delphi?

ORACLE OF DELPHI: If yes, yes, and if no, no.

NATHAN: I do not understand your answer.

ORACLE OF DELPHI: What answer don't you understand?

NATHAN: Your answer.

ORACLE OF DELPHI: What is my answer?

NATHAN: You confuse me.

ORACLE OF DELPHI: What is confusion?

NATHAN: I do not understand you.

ORACLE OF DELPHI: What is there for humans to understand?

NATHAN: Let me try again.

ORACLE OF DELPHI: Try as much as you would like.

NATHAN: I want to ask you a simple question.

ORACLE OF DELPHI: Simple is beyond human understanding.

NATHAN: Are you the Oracle of Delphi?

ORACLE OF DELPHI: Some people say I am.

NATHAN: Now we are making some progress.

ORACLE OF DELPHI: So you say.

NATHAN: I want to ask you about three meetings you had with Oedipus and members of his family.

ORACLE OF DELPHI: Three is more than two and less than four.

NATHAN: Let us start with the first meeting.

ORACLE OF DELPHI: First is first.

NATHAN: Many years ago, did Laius, the father of Oedipus come to you?

ORACLE OF DELPHI: So you say.

NATHAN: Did you tell him that his newborn son would kill him upon reaching man's estate and marry his mother?

ORACLE OF DELPHI: If I did, I did, and if not, not.

NATHAN: Why would you tell him something so heinous?

ORACLE OF DELPHI: Because it would happen.

NATHAN: How did you know it would happen?

ORACLE OF DELPHI: Because it was prophesied.

NATHAN: Was there nothing that could be done to prevent it?

ORACLE OF DELPHI: Nothing.

NATHAN: But because of this, Laius arranged with his wife to expose Oedipus on the mountain range and leave him to die.

ORACLE OF DELPHI: It didn't matter what he had done or did. It was prophesied and man cannot escape his fate.

NATHAN: But this set in motion the entire process where Oedipus was raised by his adopted father, King Polybus of Corinth and his wife, the Dorian Merope.

ORACLE OF DELPHI: There was nothing to set in motion. Don't you understand, this was prophesied and I was simply the voice transmitting the information.

NATHAN: Don't you see that your words made Oedipus an unwanted child?

ORACLE OF DELPHI: Again, I was simply the voice transmitting what would happen.

NATHAN: Do you not see the damage in what you did and the suffering you brought?

ORACLE OF DELPHI: There is no man not born to suffering.

NATHAN: Let me proceed to the second meeting.

ORACLE OF DELPHI: Second is not first.

NATHAN: Did Oedipus, now grown, come to you and ask you questions about his identity?

ORACLE OF DELPHI: What do you mean, "identity"?

NATHAN: Who his parents were?

ORACLE OF DELPHI: I seem to remember something like this.

NATHAN: What did you answer?

ORACLE OF DELPHI: What did I answer?

NATHAN: That he was destined to kill his father and marry his mother.

ORACLE OF DELPHI: So you say.

NATHAN: Why did you answer in this way?

ORACLE OF DELPHI: Because it was prophesied.

NATHAN: But this was not the question Oedipus asked you.

ORACLE OF DELPHI: Now it is I who don't understand you.

NATHAN: Did Oedipus not ask you who his parents were?

ORACLE OF DELPHI: So you say.

NATHAN: But you didn't answer his question?

ORACLE OF DELPHI: What would you have had me answer him?

NATHAN: Who his parents were.

ORACLE OF DELPHI: But I did answer him. I told him he was destined to kill his father and marry his mother.

NATHAN: But you never told him who his biological parents were, and by not telling him this, you brought about the very events you were warning him against.

ORACLE OF DELPHI: Don't you understand that this was prophesied?

NATHAN: But your misleading answer brought it about .You entrapped him.

ORACLE OF DELPHI: What would you have had me answer him.

NATHAN: That since he was destined to kill his father and marry his mother, he should stay in Corinth where his adopted father and mother were.

ORACLE OF DELPHI: Don't you understand? No human can escape his destiny.

NATHAN: Let me now move ahead to the third meeting.

ORACLE OF DELPHI: Third is not second or first.

NATHAN: Did Creon come to ask you about the cause of the pestilence in Thebes?

ORACLE OF DELPHI: You seem to know all, yet nothing.

NATHAN: What did you answer him?

ORACLE OF DELPHI: I think you know the answer.

NATHAN: Did you answer him that the plague was occurring because the killer of Laius was in Thebes polluting the land?

ORACLE OF DELPHI: Yes.

NATHAN: Why did you answer in this way?

ORACLE OF DELPHI: Because it was prophesied.

NATHAN: But your actions helped bring this about.

ORACLE OF DELPHI: I am simply an oracle. I bring nothing about. I simply report what is prophesied.

NATHAN: But your actions brought this about.

ORACLE OF DELPHI: I brought nothing about. I simply report what is prophesied. Man cannot escape his fate.

NATHAN: Thank you.

NATHAN (to Nasi): I am finished questioning this witness.

NASI: This witness is open for questioning by members of the Sanhedrin.

SAGE 1: I am simply aghast. You talk as if life is a closed circle and there is nothing anyone can do to change anything.

ORACLE OF DELPHI: No one can change his destiny.

SAGE 2: Do you believe that even your gods cannot change destiny?

ORACLE OF DELPHI: No. They too are governed by fate and necessity.

SAGE 3: But what if one does act in the manner that you say?

ORACLE OF DELPHI: This was ordained.

SAGE 3: But what if one does the opposite of what you say?

ORACLE OF DELPHI: Then that was ordained.

SAGE 4: Then, if all is pre-ordained, how can one hold Oedipus guilty for what transpired in Thebes?

ORACLE OF DELPHI: Because he was a pollutant of the land.

NASI *(to the Sanhedrin):* Do you have any more questions for this witness?

No response from the Sanhedrin.

NASI: In this case, the court will adjourn overnight and begin the closing arguments in the morning.

SCENE 8

Sophocles sees Nathan at same café as in Act II Scene 3

Sophocles enters the café and sees Nathan sitting at a table drinking tea. He approaches Nathan's table and asks Nathan if he may join him.

SOPHOCLES: May I join you?

NATHAN: Of course.

SOPHOCLES: It has been a very interesting trial.

NATHAN: Yes, it has been.

SOPHOCLES (*sitting down*): I am quite exhausted from it.

NATHAN: I am also.

SOPHOCLES: We are not allowed to talk about the trial. I am too tired to talk about it in any case.

NATHAN: What do you do in your daily life?

SOPHOCLES: I am a playwright.

NATHAN: What is a playwright?

SOPHOCLES: A person who writes plays.

NATHAN: What is a play?

SOPHOCLES: A set of events and conversations that are performed by actors.

NATHAN: About what?

SOPHOCLES: About events in the lives of people.

NATHAN: Real events? Events that actually happened to people?

SOPHOCLES: They could be, or they could be based on myths. Are dramatic plays not performed in Judea?

NATHAN: Not like the plays you mentioned a moment ago.

SOPHOCLES: Then what do people do here to learn about life?

NATHAN: They read the Torah, the Hebrew Scriptures.

SOPHOCLES: What is that?

NATHAN: It is the history of Israel from the beginning of time.

SOPHOCLES: So is it not mythology?

NATHAN: No. It is our history.

SOPHOCLES: We have our great historians as well, Thucydides and Herodotus, to name two.

NATHAN: The Torah is more than history.

SOPHOCLES: What more is it.

NATHAN: It is the story of the encounter of *HaShem*, our God, with his people Israel.

SOPHOCLES: I am not certain I understand, but no matter. What is it you do, Nathan?

NATHAN: I have been told I am a prophet.

SOPHOCLES: So you are like our Teiresias, foretelling the future?

NATHAN: Not exactly.

SOPHOCLES: So then what exactly do you do?

NATHAN: I warn people of impending disaster unless they change their ways.

SOPHOCLES: But is this not predicting the future?

NATHAN: No, people can avert disaster by changing their behavior, and hence change the future.

SOPHOCLES: I don't understand, but no matter. I am tired now and I am going to rest. I will see you in court tomorrow.

NATHAN: Good night, Adoni.

SCENE 9

The closing arguments

The next morning. The Court reconvenes. Oedipus sits with his gag taken off. Sophocles and Nathan approach the Nasi.

NASI *(to Sophocles and Nathan)*: Are you prepared to present summary arguments?

SOPHOCLES: I am, your honor.

NATHAN: I also.

NASI *(to Sophocles)*: You may proceed.

SOPHOCLES: Esteemed court, I will be brief. I have presented witnesses of the case against King Oedipus. It is compelling. Witnesses have identified Oedipus as being the son of King Laius and Queen Jocasta. Another witness has identified Oedipus as murdering his father, King Laius. He subsequently lay in sinful matrimony with his widowed mother Jocasta, begetting children with her who are his siblings. He has admitted this, as demonstrated by his taking out of his eyes.

    This poor man is guilty of the worst pollution possible and has continuously shouted out and admitted his guilt in this Sanhedrin. He admits he has taken out his eyes to cut himself off from all contact with humanity. Incest is incest and creates a pollution that must be removed. He agrees that he is cursed by the gods because of the great pollution he has caused, which cannot be forgiven. Oedipus is guilty of patricide and incest with his mother.

OEDIPUS *(screaming)*: I am the worst of all people, the most guilty of all. I have no place in this world. I have polluted all that it is holy. I am cursed and deserve all that has happened to me.

Oedipus is re-gagged.

SOPHOCLES: This is my summary argument of the case against Oedipus. Let not compassion for this miserable man obscure the fact that his heinous acts cannot be forgiven and that he has polluted the land in which he was born and has acted as a king. He is cursed by men and gods.

NASI: Have you completed your argument?

SOPHOCLES: I have.

NASI *(looking at Nathan)*: Is the defense ready to make its summary argument?

NATHAN: I am.

Oedipus is ungagged.

NATHAN: Dear sages, I too will be brief. It is clear that this man Oedipus is absolutely innocent of the charges leveled against him. Oedipus had absolutely no knowledge that he had murdered his biological father and in fact he did everything he could to avoid this. On the contrary, it is Laius who tried to kill the infant Oedipus by ordering his servant to leave the infant on a mountain top to die. All of this, because Laius had heard from the Oracle of Delphi that Oedipus was destined to kill him when Oedipus became a man.

The very idea of a father killing his son is anathema to the Jewish tradition. The entire experience of God staying Abraham's hand to prevent him from slaying his son Isaac in Genesis 22:11-12 is an absolute rebuke to the practices of worshipers of the cult of the god Moloch who did sacrifice their children. Of course, this was forbidden by G-d's word recorded in Leviticus 18:21, "Neither shall you give any of your offspring to offer them to Moloch, nor shall you profane the name of your G-d; I am the Lord." Indeed our tradition commands the father to teach his son thoroughly in Deuteronomy 6:7 and in Kiddushin 30a.

The oracle's words are sad and vicious, reflecting a profound and deadly fear of the future. The infant Oedipus survives only because of the kindness of the shepherd in the adjoining field who brought the infant to his own master, King Polybus of Corinth, who raises Oedipus as his own son, whom Oedipus thought he was. Oedipus does not have the slightest intention of killing the man he thought to be his father. This is evidenced by Oedipus' actions when he hears from the Oracle of Delphi that he is destined to kill his father and marry his mother. Confused, and not wanting to insult or question the man Oedipus thinks to be his father and the woman he thinks to be his mother, he flees Corinth.

Through perverse circumstances, he slays a man while defending himself during a quarrel on the road to Thebes. This man happens to be Laius, the biological father of Oedipus, but it is clear that Oedipus did not know this. After this, Oedipus rescues Thebes from the Sphinx that has been terrorizing it. As a reward, Oedipus is given Jocasta, the widow of Laius, to be his wife and Oedipus is made King of Thebes. By all accounts, he is an excellent, responsible ruler. Together, Jocasta and Oedipus have four children, but neither Jocasta nor Oedipus knows that they are mother and son.

In my own life, I confronted our own King David with a parable after he committed adultery with Bathsheba, the wife of one of his officers, and intentionally arranged to have that officer, Uriah, placed in the battlefield to be killed. I confronted David about this through a parable, not one of these miserable riddles, to make him understand what he had done. David realizes what he had intentionally done, sincerely atoned before *HaShem*, and ultimately is forgiven. King David's actions are much worse than those of Oedipus. Yet King David atoned and was ultimately forgiven.

Why is not Oedipus given a chance to atone for an act that was not intentional?

The patricide and incest committed by Oedipus were wholly unintentional, brought about by vicious riddles and misleading and entrapping information. The terrible acts that occur after Jocasta and Oedipus realize they are mother and son are totally unnecessary. There is absolutely no reason that Oedipus and Jocasta could not have gone on with their lives, having raised four beautiful children. Oedipus had done nothing wrong and is innocent of both charges. Oedipus is innocent. What should be brought to trial here is the entire Greek conception of fate, *moira*, and necessity, *ananke*, which reduces man to a mere shell, an automaton, and strips him of the free will and dignity which *HaShem* has given him, by making him in His own image.

OEDIPUS *(again screaming)*: I am the worst of all people, the most guilty of all. I have no place in this world. I have polluted all that it is holy. I am cursed and deserve all that has happened to me.

Oedipus is re-gagged.

NATHAN: This is my summary argument in defense of Oedipus against the charges of patricide and incest. He has been done in by a set of circumstances engendered by incomplete and misleading information. Let us not compound the damage done to him by declaring him guilty for crimes he did not knowingly commit. Let the court show compassion for this man and realize he has been an innocent pawn in this whole sad episode.

NASI: The court is cleared while the members of the Sanhedrin discuss the verdict.

SCENE 10

The decision of the Sanhedrin

The Sanhedrin is reconvened. Oedipus is ungagged.

NASI: I have received a note from the Sanhedrin that they have arrived at a verdict. Is this correct?

SPOKESMAN FOR THE SANHEDRIN: We have. We would like to offer our verdict and the reasoning behind it.

NASI: What is your verdict?

SPOKESMAN FOR THE SANHEDRIN: We find Oedipus not guilty of the crimes of patricide and incest.

NASI: Can you state your reasoning?

SPOKESMAN FOR THE SANHEDRIN: Sometimes complicated occurrences happen in a person's or a people's history. The Torah, for example portrays several stories of incest, all intentional, at least on the part of the younger parties with the intention of ensuring their future. For example, after the destruction of Sodom, Lot's daughters think that their father is the last man in the world. They get him drunk and lie with him to ensure the future. This is purposeful incest on their part. Indeed this is what the name *Moab* signifies: "from the father." Yet from this union, several generations later, come good things: Ruth who becomes a great heroine of the Jewish people, a devoted daughter, wife and mother, and the ancestress of King David. Another story of incest involves Tamar with Judah, her father-in-law. This too is done to ensure the future of the tribe of Judah.

We reason from these cases that even intentional incest can sometimes be forgiven, if the aim is positive towards embracing the future. The incest in the case of Oedipus is totally unintentional and prompted by fear of the future. Deep in our own tradition is the belief that each generation is a link in a chain between the generation coming before and that coming after. A father wants his son to surpass him. Yet King Laius hears from the Oracle of Delphi the obscene prophecy that his infant son Oedipus will kill him upon reaching man's estate and will marry his mother.

This pronouncement of the oracle is sick to its core. It is made abundantly clear in our tradition that child-sacrifice is forbidden. Genesis 22:11-12 clearly states the Angel of the Lord staying Abraham's hand on Mount Moriah: "Do not lay your hand on the lad, nor do anything to him." More than that, we are taught in Malachi 3:23-24 that the father must come to love his son and the son, his father. "And he shall turn the hearts of the fathers to the children, the hearts of the children to their fathers; lest I come and smite the land with utter destruction." Further, a father is commanded to teach his son thoroughly at Deuteronomy 6:7 and Kiddushin, 30a. The father's identity is not threatened by his son. He wants to see his son develop and surpass him.

The oracle's prophesy turns on its head a healthy relationship between father and son to a competitive murderous one. This sets in motion a lethal identity confusion leading to Oedipus' patricide and incest, of which he was unaware. Let us review the steps in this terrible and unnecessary tragedy enveloping a decent man trying to do the right thing.

First, the Oracle's pronouncement produces in Oedipus the status of an unwanted child.

Second, Laius attempts to kill his son.

Third, as a direct result of Laius' attempt to kill his son, Oedipus is rescued and adopted by King Polybus of Corinth.

Fourth, Oedipus grows up thinking Polybus is his father and Merope his mother.

Fifth, Oedipus overhears a man questioning his identity

Sixth, Confused, Oedipus goes to the Oracle to seek information about his parentage.

Seventh, The Oracle does not answer this question. Instead, she tells Oedipus that he is fated to kill his father and marry his mother.

Eighth, Oedipus becomes frightened and flees from Corinth to avoid hurting his supposed parents.

Ninth, Oedipus kills an older man in self-defense over a quarrel regarding right-of-way at a crossing on the road to Thebes. Oedipus does not know that man was his biological father. Indeed, he thinks King Polybus of Corinth is his biological father.

Tenth, Oedipus correctly solves the riddle of the Sphinx which is terrorizing Thebes. But despite the fact that Oedipus is highly intelligent, he remains trapped by the paralysis of Greek fatalism.

Eleventh, in response to this, Oedipus is rewarded with the Kingship of Thebes and is wed to Queen Jocasta, the widow of King Laius. There is not the slightest shred of evidence that Oedipus has any sense that she is his mother. Indeed, he thinks that the Dorian Merope, the wife of King Polybus, is his biological mother.

OEDIPUS (*ungagged, yells*): Incest is incest. And it creates a pollution that must be removed.

Oedipus is re-gagged.

SPOKESMAN FOR THE SANHEDRIN (*continues*): There is no such thing as fate. Free will has been given to people by our

Creator. Oedipus has tortured himself needlessly. Oedipus is not strictly speaking a tragic figure, because he has not been done in by any character flaw on his part, but because of a confusion in his identity resulting from his status as an unwanted child. Oedipus has been entrapped by a vicious series of partial and confusing information and sadistic riddles which has been misleadingly called "fate." He has tortured himself needlessly. And this indeed is what is tragic.

OEDIPUS *(pulls off his gag and shouts)*: No, I am a pollutant, the worst of the worst.

SPOKESMAN FOR THE SANHEDRIN *(continues)*: This Greek idea is not an organic living morality nor does it represent a truly human justice. It is only an abstract mathematics, a bloodless geometry of ideal forms which do not exist in reality. It seems to us that it is not Oedipus who is guilty but an entire way of thinking, one which uses incomplete information and riddling to make it impossible for a person to exercise the free will given to him by his creator.

NASI: Do you then not find Oedipus guilty of any crime?

SPOKESMAN FOR THE SANHEDRIN: Only one act, esteemed sir, an act he has not been accused of.

AV BET DIN: If he has not been accused, this court cannot find Oedipus guilty, and no punishment can be assessed.

SPOKESMAN FOR THE SANHEDRIN: We understand this, Adoni. Yet this act is so destructive, we must comment on it.

VICE-PRESIDENT OF THE SANHEDRIN: And what is this act?

SPOKESMAN FOR THE SANHEDRIN: Oedipus' taking out his eyes. The prohibition against self-injury occurs in Deuteronomy 14:1 in our Holy Torah. "Ye are the children of the Lord your G-d. You shall not cut yourself nor make any baldness between your eyes for the dead."

NASI: The Sanhedrin will note this. The Sanhedrin finds Oedipus not guilty of intentional patricide or incest, yet expresses its dismay and horror over his self-mutilation. The trial of Oedipus is completed. The Sanhedrin is adjourned.

OEDIPUS *(continues to shout):* I am guilty! I am guilty! I am guilty of patricide and incest. I am a pollutant, the worst of the worst.

End of Play